This book belongs to

A Read-Aloud Storybook

Adapted by
Christine Peymani

Illustrated by
Caroline Egan, Adrienne Brown, Scott Tilley, and Studio IBOIX

Designed by
Deborah Boone

Published in the United States by Random House Children's Books, a division of Random House, Inc.,
1745 Broadway, New York, NY 10019, and in Canada by Random House of Canada Limited, Toronto, in conjunction with
Disney Enterprises, Inc. Random House and the colophon are registered trademarks of Random House, Inc.
Library of Congress Control Number: 2009935751
ISBN: 978-0-7364-2709-8
www.randomhouse.com/kids
Printed in the United States of America
10 9 8 7 6 5 4 3 2 1

Sheriff Woody was in the middle of another exciting adventure. He had made his way to the top of a thundering train, where he battled the villainous One-Eyed Bart. But Woody wasn't alone—Bullseye the horse and Jessie the yodeling cowgirl were galloping nearby, ready to help. Still, all might have been lost without the swooping strength of Buzz Lightyear, Space Ranger!

But the fight wasn't over. One-Eyed Bart and the evil Dr. Porkchop struck back—attacking with their force-field dog and a pack of Aliens.

By working together, the unstoppable Sheriff Woody and Buzz Lightyear saved the day at last!

When Andy was young, his toys had enjoyed exciting adventures every day. Andy's imagination could take them anywhere—the future, the past, deserts, jungles, and distant planets.

Andy loved his toys. And Woody, Buzz, Jessie, Rex, Hamm, Slinky Dog, and the rest of the toy gang loved him right back. For the toys, being played with—and being loved—by a kid was the best feeling in the whole world.

The years went by. Andy grew up into a teenager and played with his toys less and less. Feeling neglected, the toys finally came up with a plan to get Andy's attention.

First, Sarge and his troop of toy soldiers crept through the house and nabbed Andy's cell phone. Then they hauled it back to the toy box. Once the cell phone was hidden inside, Jessie turned to a nearby cordless phone. She began pressing numbers as the others gathered around nervously.

The cell phone started ringing. Suddenly, Andy's footsteps pounded up the stairs as he approached the toy box. The toys held still as he reached inside and pulled out his phone.

"Hello . . . ? Anyone there?" Andy asked. But no one answered.

The toys held their breath. Would he play with them?

"Molly, stay out of my room!" Andy shouted to his little sister. Then he rolled his eyes and closed the lid on his old friends.

After Andy was gone, the toys spilled out of the toy box, feeling disappointed. In a few days, Andy would go to college. That meant playtime was over—maybe forever.

Then Buzz noticed Sarge preparing to parachute out the window. "What are you doing?" Buzz asked.

"When the trash bags come out, we Army guys are the first to go," one soldier replied.

Trash bags? The other toys started squeaking and shouting, terrified at the idea of being thrown out.

"Hold on!" shouted Woody. He reminded them that through the years, Andy had always kept them. "He must care about us, or we wouldn't still be here," Woody reasoned. They'd just be put into the attic, where they could all be together.

"I'd better find my other eye," said Mrs. Potato Head. She sighed as the toys all gathered their parts together and got ready for the attic.

Just then, the toys heard someone coming. They scrambled back into the toy box as Andy came into the room. His mom followed—carrying trash bags! She reminded Andy that he needed to begin sorting his things.

She also told Molly to donate some of her toys to the Sunnyside Daycare center. Turning to Andy, she asked if he wanted to donate his old toys as well.

Andy shook his head. "No one's going to want those old toys," he told her. "They're junk."

Inside the toy box, the toys felt hurt. Did Andy really think they were junk?

They were even more upset when Andy started scooping them up and dumping them into a trash bag!

But when he picked up Woody and Buzz, he paused. They had always been his two favorites. He looked back and forth between them, then made his decision. Buzz went into the trash bag. Woody went into a box marked COLLEGE.

Buzz couldn't believe this was happening!

Woody couldn't believe it, either. As Andy carried the bag away, Woody followed him into the hallway. Then Andy pulled down the ladder to the attic. Whew! Everyone would be safe after all.

But just as Andy started up the ladder, Molly called him. Andy left the trash bag in the hall. When his mom walked by moments later, she grabbed the bag and carried it out of the house.

She was *throwing the toys away!*

Andy's mom tossed the bag onto the sidewalk, by the garbage cans.

The toys began to panic. "There's got to be a way out!" shouted Buzz, looking around desperately. Finally, he had an idea: they could use Rex's pointy tail to tear through the bag.

Everyone pushed Rex against the plastic as hard as they could, but they were running out of time. "I can hear the garbage truck!" Rex cried.

Watching from the window, Woody was frantic! He grabbed a pair of scissors, climbed out the window, and raced to the pile of trash. He sliced open one bag after another. Where were his friends?

Moments later, the garbage truck arrived. The neighborhood trash collector hurled all the bags into the truck. Then the truck rumbled off, leaving Woody sad and alone.

Just then, Woody noticed an upside-down recycling bin making its way across Andy's driveway. His friends had escaped!

Inside the garage, the toys were in an uproar.

"Andy threw us out!" exclaimed Slinky Dog.

"Like we were garbage!" added Hamm.

Luckily, Jessie had a plan. By the time Woody reached the garage, she and the other toys were all climbing into the donation box for Sunnyside Daycare.

Woody tried to explain that Andy didn't mean to throw them out. But the toys weren't convinced. Then, suddenly, Andy's mom slammed the hatchback shut.

As they drove to Sunnyside, Woody told his friends that daycare was a sad, lonely place. "You'll be begging to go home," he warned.

But when the car pulled up in front of Sunnyside, it didn't seem sad at all. The building looked cheerful, and children laughed and played outside. The toys could hardly contain their excitement—maybe they would get played with again!

Once inside the building, the toys got so excited that they accidentally knocked the box over.

A crowd of daycare toys swarmed around them. "Welcome to Sunnyside!" a big pink bear called warmly. "I'm Lots-o'-Huggin' Bear! But please, call me Lotso!"

After everything they had been through that day, the toys were happy to see a friendly face.

"Mr. Lotso," asked Rex. "Do toys here get played with every day?"

"All day long. Five days a week," Lotso replied.

"But what happens when the kids grow up?" Jessie wanted to know.

"When the kids get old, new ones come in," Lotso told her. "You'll never be outgrown or neglected. Never abandoned or forgotten. No owners means no heartbreak."

To Andy's toys, Sunnyside sounded like a dream come true!

"Now let's get you all settled in," Lotso said.

The friendly bear led everyone on a complete tour of the daycare center. By the time they reached the Caterpillar Room, their new home, Andy's toys were amazed. Sunnyside seemed to have everything they needed!

But one toy wasn't completely won over by Sunnyside. Woody reminded Buzz and the others that they were still Andy's toys. Sunnyside might be nice, but it wasn't home.

"We can have a new life here, Woody," Jessie argued. "A chance to make kids happy again."

"So this is it?" Woody asked. "After all we've been through?" No one answered, so Woody walked away—all by himself.

Woody slipped out of the Caterpillar Room just as the janitor was passing by. Woody jumped onto the rolling trash can and hopped off at the bathroom. Then he climbed through a window and onto the roof.

But how would he get over the tall wall that surrounded the daycare center?

Luckily, Woody spotted an old kite on the roof. Holding it above his head, he leaped off the roof and soared over the wall!

But instead of gliding down, Woody flew upward on a gust of wind!

Suddenly, the kite snapped, and the cowboy tumbled down into a tree. His hat fell to the sidewalk, and his pull string caught on a branch, leaving him dangling above the ground.

At that moment, a little girl named Bonnie spotted him. She was just leaving the daycare center to go home. Bonnie reached up, stuffed Woody into her backpack, and climbed into her mom's waiting car.

Woody was glad to be rescued—but he still needed to get home to Andy!

Back in the Caterpillar Room, Andy's toys waited eagerly as they heard the children approaching. Suddenly, a crowd of energetic toddlers burst into the room. The children grabbed the toys, shrieking happily.

But this playtime was not what the toys expected. The toddlers tangled Slinky's coil, broke off Rex's tail, and used Buzz as a hammer!

One of the toddlers threw Buzz into the air, and he landed beside a window that looked into the daycare center's other classroom. There, in the Butterfly Room, Buzz saw a group of preschoolers playing gently with Lotso and other daycare toys.

There must have been a mistake! Why weren't Buzz and his friends in the Butterfly Room, too? *That* was where they should be—not in the chaos of the Caterpillar Room.

Meanwhile, Woody was having a very different experience at Bonnie's house.

The little girl loved to play, and happily launched into an amazing game of make-believe, the best Woody had enjoyed in years! After Bonnie left the room, though, Woody quickly explained his situation to the other toys. Buttercup the unicorn and Mr. Pricklepants the hedgehog were very kind, but Woody still wanted to get home to Andy.

Back at Sunnyside, the toys were exhausted and sore. "These toddlers!" exclaimed Mr. Potato Head. "They don't know how to play with us!"

Buzz decided to talk to Lotso about being moved to the big-kids' room. But the doors and windows were locked! Luckily, Buzz found one open window at the top of the door. He scrambled out to find the pink bear.

Buzz found Lotso's crew in the teachers' lounge, inside the top of a snack machine.

"What do you guys think of the new recruits?" Buzz heard someone ask. "Any keepers?"

"All of them toys are disposable," replied the toy named Twitch. "We'll be lucky if they last us a week!"

Buzz was shocked. Lotso had put Andy's toys in the Caterpillar Room on purpose! Buzz whirled around, anxious to warn his friends—and ran right into the gigantic doll named Big Baby.

Back in the Caterpillar Room, Mrs. Potato Head gasped suddenly. "I see Andy!" she cried. But she wasn't seeing the daycare center. Mrs. Potato Head was seeing Andy's house through the eye she had accidentally left there!

Andy seemed upset. "Andy's looking for us! I think he did mean to put us in the attic!" Mrs. Potato Head said.

The toys realized that Woody had been right. They needed to go home to Andy right away!

Down the hall, Buzz demanded to talk to Lotso. The pink bear was friendly at first.

But when Buzz explained that he and his friends belonged in the Butterfly Room, Lotso stopped being nice. "Those Caterpillar kids need someone to play with," he growled. He wanted Andy's toys to stay with the little kids so he wouldn't have to!

Lotso strapped Buzz to a chair and prepared to switch the space ranger back to his original factory setting.

"Nooooo!" Buzz yelled.

Not long after, Lotso entered the Caterpillar Room. Andy's toys hurried over to explain that they had been donated by accident and needed to get home right away.

"You ain't leavin' Sunnyside," Lotso snarled.

Out of the shadows, Buzz appeared. For a moment, his friends were relieved. But then they noticed his blank stare. Suddenly, Buzz went into karate mode and knocked Jessie and the others to the ground.

"Silence, minions of Zurg!" he shouted. "You're in the custody of the Galactic Alliance!"

Lotso's gang herded Andy's toys into storage cubbies and trapped them inside. "We've got a way of doing things here at Sunnyside," Lotso explained. "Life here can be a dream come true. But if you break the rules . . ." The pink bear threw Woody's hat on the floor in front of them. Then he chuckled wickedly as he walked out.

Buzz saluted Lotso, then turned and glared at his horrified prisoners. There would be no escapees on his watch.

Meanwhile, Woody had discovered that he was only a few blocks from Andy's house! As he prepared to leave, Woody told Bonnie's toys that his friends were still at Sunnyside.

"Sunnyside?!" an old clown toy named Chuckles gasped. A long time ago, Chuckles, Lotso, and Big Baby had all belonged to a little girl named Daisy. Unfortunately, they were accidentally left behind during a trip. By the time they finally made their way home, Daisy owned a new Lots-o'-Huggin' Bear. Lotso told Big Baby that Daisy didn't love them anymore.

The toys wandered aimlessly until they reached Sunnyside. But Lotso's heart had hardened. Since then, he had ruled Sunnyside with a furry iron paw. New toys didn't stand a chance.

Woody felt torn. Andy was leaving for college the next day. And if Woody wasn't in the COLLEGE box, he might never see his best friend again. But he knew he couldn't leave Buzz, Jessie, and the others in Lotso's clutches!

The next morning, Woody stowed away in Bonnie's backpack when she left for Sunnyside. After Bonnie hung up her backpack, Woody crawled out and sneaked over to the Caterpillar Room.

Woody's friends were overjoyed to see him. They handed his hat back to him with relieved smiles. "Oh, Woody," cried Jessie, "we were wrong to leave Andy!"

"From now on, we stick together," Woody replied.

Everyone knew that Woody needed to get home quickly so he could go to college with Andy. Luckily, Woody had a plan. He pointed out the window at the trash chute. That would be their escape route!

That night, the toys put their escape plan into action. Some of them distracted Buzz while Woody and Slinky snatched the daycare center's master key.

Mr. Potato Head tossed his removable parts into the playground, where they attached themselves to a tortilla. In his new identity as Mr. Tortilla Head, he watched for Lotso and his gang.

Jessie unlocked the door and led Andy's toys out onto the playground, while Rex and Hamm tried to reset Buzz.

Suddenly, Buzz beeped—and began speaking Spanish!

Woody tried to hustle Buzz along, but when the space ranger saw Jessie, he dropped to his knees. *"¡Mi florecita del desierto!"* he declared romantically.

"Did you fix Buzz?" asked Jessie, confused.

"Sort of," Woody replied.

Soon Mr. Tortilla Head joined them as well. In no time, he was reunited with his old potato body—and a very relieved Mrs. Potato Head.

Together, the friends crept past Big Baby and across the playground, avoiding a spotlight that swept over the yard. Quickly, the group headed toward the trash chute.

Woody slid down the chute, then called for his friends to follow. Soon they were all outside, perched above an open Dumpster.

Slinky stretched himself across the Dumpster so that the toys could climb across to safety.

But suddenly, Lotso stepped into view. “You lost, little doggie?” he asked with a nasty grin. Lotso kicked Slinky’s paws, almost knocking the dog into the trash below.

"Why don't you come back and join our family again?" Lotso asked the toys.

"You're a liar and a bully and I'd rather rot in this Dumpster than join any family of yours!" Jessie declared.

Lotso glared at her. "I didn't throw you away," he replied. "Your kid did. There isn't one kid who ever loved a toy, really."

"What about Daisy?" Woody demanded. "She lost you. By accident." He held up a pendant Chuckles had given him—long ago, it had belonged to Big Baby. It read: MY HEART BELONGS TO DAISY.

My Heart Belongs To:
DAISY

"She never loved me!" Lotso shouted. "She left me!"

Big Baby stepped toward the pendant and picked it up. His eyes filled with tears as he remembered Daisy. "Mama!" he cried sadly.

Lotso shoved Big Baby. "You want your mommy back?"

Furious, Big Baby picked Lotso up, threw him into the Dumpster, and shut the lid! Then, at last, Big Baby smiled. Lotso couldn't bully anyone anymore.

The toys could hear a garbage truck approaching as they hurried across the Dumpster. Everyone made it—except for one Alien, whose foot got caught.

Woody ran back to help, but Lotso reached up and grabbed his ankle!

Jessie, Buzz, and the rest of Andy's toys tried to help. But just then, the garbage truck arrived. The Dumpster was lifted into the air, and everyone—including Lotso—tumbled into the back of the truck.

Inside, Woody heard the truck starting to pick up another Dumpster. "Against the wall! Quick!" he shouted.

Jessie was caught under some trash, so Buzz raced over to free her. He pushed her safely out of the path of falling garbage. Just then a TV dropped directly on top of Buzz!

Quickly, his friends dug the space ranger out, hoping he was okay. In fact, he was better than okay. The bump had knocked Buzz out of Spanish mode—he was himself again!

At the garbage dump, the truck dumped its load of trash. Dirty and frightened, the toys struggled free.

In the distance, they cou ld see the silhouette of a huge crane. "The Claaaaw!" shouted the Aliens excitedly, toddling off toward it.

Woody tried to stop them, but a bulldozer cut him off. The toys were pushed along, caught in a churning tide of smelly garbage.

The toys tumbled down onto a conveyor belt. Suddenly, a big magnet began pulling metal from the trash. Slinky was pulled up first—and he could see that his friends were heading toward a shredder! The rest of the toys grabbed whatever metal they could find and were pulled up by the powerful magnet.

Suddenly, a pink paw reached out from under a golf bag. "Help!" begged Lotso.

Woody and Buzz pried the bag off with a golf club, then pointed the metal club upward. All three toys were lifted into the air just in the nick of time.

Everyone cheered to see that Lotso was safe. "Thank you, Sheriff," Lotso said humbly.

"We're all in this together," replied Woody.

Unfortunately, the new conveyor wasn't truly safe—it led to a flaming incinerator! Lotso spotted an emergency stop button, and the others boosted him up to reach it.

Lotso was about to push the button. But as he looked at the other toys, his expression hardened again. Instead of saving them, he ran away!

Terrified, the toys tumbled toward the fiery blaze. It looked as if there was no escape. They held each other's hands, together till the end.

Suddenly, a giant crane came down. Its jaws opened, scooping them away from the inferno!

As they soared through the air, the toys could see the Aliens at the controls of the crane! "The Claaaaw!" the Aliens cried joyfully.

The Aliens set the toys gently on the ground.

"Come on, Woody," said Jessie. "We've got to get you home."

Fortunately, their neighborhood garbage collector was just climbing into his truck. The toys jumped aboard, eager to hitch a ride.

Behind them, Lotso was going somewhere, too. A different truck driver had found him and happily tied the pink bear to the front grille of his garbage truck. "I had me one o' these when I was a kid!" the driver exclaimed.

Woody and the gang arrived home as Andy was loading up the car. They were just in time.

After hosing themselves off in the yard, the toys sneaked back into Andy's room. As soon as they were inside, Mrs. Potato Head picked up her missing eye from under the bed. She was happy to be all together again!

As the other toys climbed into the box marked ATTIC, Woody and Buzz shook hands.

After so many adventures together, the two friends couldn't believe they were parting. "This isn't goodbye," Woody said.

Finally, Buzz turned to go. "You know where to find us, cowboy," he said, climbing into the ATTIC box with the rest of the toys.

While Andy finished packing, Woody gazed at a photo of Andy with his toys. Then he watched as Andy and his mom said goodbye to each other. Woody realized that he and Andy would always have memories of their time together, too. No matter what happened, they'd never really lose each other.

Suddenly, Woody knew what he had to do. He scribbled something on a sticky note, then stuck the note on the ATTIC box.

When Andy returned, he was thrilled to see his toys! He'd thought they were gone forever. Then he looked at the sticky note.

"Hey, Mom," he called. "So you really think I should donate these?"

"It's up to you, honey," she replied.

Andy loaded the box into his car and drove to the address written on the sticky note. It was a small house with a little girl playing out front. It was Bonnie's house!

Andy pulled his toys from the box and introduced each one to Bonnie. And at the bottom of the box, there was Woody! Andy was surprised—Woody was supposed to go to college with him. But Bonnie recognized Woody immediately. "My cowboy!" she exclaimed. When Andy saw how much Bonnie loved Woody, he decided to leave his favorite toy with her, too.

Then Andy played with Bonnie and all his old toys. After so many years, Woody, Buzz, and the others were finally getting what they wanted: one last playtime with Andy.

Back in the car, Andy took a last look at Bonnie, surrounded by his toys. "Bye, guys," he said quietly.

Bonnie ran inside for lunch, leaving the toys alone to watch Andy drive away.

"So long, partner," said Woody with a wave.

Buzz put his arm around Woody. Yes, their life with Andy was ending. But their adventures with Bonnie had just begun.